Published by Ladybird Books Ltd
A Penguin Company
Penguin Books Ltd, 80 Strand, London, WC2R 0RL, England
Penguin Books Australia Ltd, Camberwell, Victoria, Australia
Penguin Group (NZ), cnr Airborne and Rosedale Roads, Albany,
Auckland 1310, New Zealand

ISBN-13: 978-1-84646-125-5
ISBN-10: 1-8464-6125-1

Manufactured in Italy

Angelina in the Wings

"I have wonderful news!" said Miss Lilly one day after class. "As you know, the famous Madame Zizi is to perform 'The Sun Queen' at the theatre!"

"And she is coming here tomorrow with
Mr Popoff, the director, to take a class
with you!"
Everyone gasped with delight.
"One of the little sunbeams in the ballet
has mousepox," Miss Lilly continued.
"Does that mean they need another
sunbeam?" asked Angelina, hardly
daring to believe it.
"It does Angelina! Indeed it does!"
smiled Miss Lilly.

That evening at supper, Cousin Henry
was running round the kitchen, playing
with his clockwork ladybird and
singing. He was very excited about
Angelina being a sunbeam.

Angelina, however, was getting nervous.
"Don't worry," said Mrs Mouseling.
"You'll have Henry as your mascot!"
"WHAT!" Angelina was horrified.
"I have to take Henry to the audition?"

"I'll be the best mascot ever!" said Henry,
spilling his drink. "What's a mascot?"
"Someone who brings luck," said Mrs
Mouseling cheerfully.
Angelina groaned.

The next day at class, Angelina felt very
nervous as she got ready. Mr Popoff was
going to take the lesson so that Madame
Zizi could watch the mouselings dance.
Henry sat at the side of the room,
playing with his ladybird and trying to
keep still.

"Alice!" whispered Angelina to her best
friend as they began to dance. "This
sunbeam is about to shine!"

As Angelina spun round the room, she hissed at Henry to sit quietly.
"Zee leetle peenk mouseling," said Madame Zizi suddenly.
"On your own please!" said Mr Popoff.

"Enchantée!" exclaimed Madame Zizi, as she watched Angelina dance on her own.

Suddenly a fly landed on Henry's nose, making him drop his ladybird!
"Oh, no!" he cried, chasing it across the floor. The ladybird bumped into Angelina, and over she toppled.
"What a sweet mouseling!" said Madame Zizi, spotting Henry. "He must be our sunbeam! Zee peenk one can understudy."

That evening, Angelina rang Alice.
"How can I get Madame Zizi to notice
me?" she cried desperately.

Henry was dancing around the room
and Mrs Mouseling came in just as he
tripped over Angelina's ballet things,
thrown carelessly on the floor. "Oh,
Angelina! I'm not your servant!"
she scolded, picking everything up.
Servant! thought Angelina.
That's a good idea!

The next day, Angelina did everything for
Madame Zizi. She ran around fetching
and carrying until she was exhausted.
Just before the rehearsal, she even helped
with her costume!

The next day, all the sunbeams, and
Angelina, danced in perfect time.
Apart from Henry.
"Jump like Angelina!" said Mr Popoff.

Henry tried hard but it was very difficult
for such a tiny mouse.
"Move back, Angelina!" continued Mr
Popoff. "They must do it alone!"

"I can't believe Henry got the part!"
sobbed Angelina that evening. "And I just
have to stand and watch! It's so unfair!"
Alice tried to comfort her.

"But when Madame Zizi sees how good you are, she's bound to make room for another sunbeam!" she said cheerily, offering Angelina a cheesy niblet.

"Where is the little boy mouseling?"
asked Mr Popoff impatiently a few
minutes later. "We are ready to start!"
Everyone looked around.
"Here I am!" sang Henry, running onto
the stage a little out of breath.
He'd got a bit lost backstage.

Madame Zizi swept him into her arms.
"Eet is not his fault," she said.
"Angelina should have been looking
after him like I told her to!"

Later, Alice tried to cheer up Angelina. "Only one more day to go then I'm a sunbeam!" smiled Henry happily. Angelina began to sob.

Then, Angelina and Alice heard Mr Popoff's voice coming from the stage. "Zizi, we have to bring on the understudy sunbeam! The boy mouseling must go!" Angelina was stunned.

"Please give him another chance," Angelina cried. "I can help him. I promise!" Madame Zizi agreed. "Yes, Popoff! You weel geev him one more chance at the dress rehearsal tomorrow. I inseest!"

That evening Angelina watched as
Henry struggled with the difficult steps.
"Well done!" she said. "Now we'll try it
again. Watch me!"

At last it was time for the dress
rehearsal. At the theatre, the sunbeams
waited in their dressing room with Mr
Popoff, ready to go on stage.

Suddenly, Madame Zizi rushed in.
"Whatever is the matter, Zizi?" asked
Mr Popoff nervously.
"Disaster!" she replied. "Another one of
our leetle sunbeams has the mousepox!"

Angelina had her chance at last!
That evening, at the performance, the
little sunbeams danced their hearts out,
and at the end proudly took their bows
behind the famous Madame Zizi.

As the performers left the stage, the applause was deafening. Mr and Mrs Mouseling, Henry's parents, Alice and Miss Lilly leapt to their feet and clapped as hard as they could.
They all felt so proud.
"Oh, Henry! You were wonderful," said Angelina breathlessly.
"You were indeed perfect, Henry," smiled Mr Popoff. "And it was all down to you, Angelina!"

The next morning, Angelina and Henry
sat side by side in bed, covered in pink
mousepox spots!
Suddenly, they heard a knock on the
bedroom door.

"Room service," laughed Mrs Mouseling, popping her head round the door. "I've brought you some cheesy niblets, sent by Alice, for two spectacular spotty sunbeams!"